Dear Parent:

Congratulations! Your child is taking the first steps on an exciting journey. The destination? Independent reading!

STEP INTO READING® will help your child get there. The program offers five steps to reading success. Each step includes fun stories and colorful art. There are also Step into Reading Sticker Books, Step into Reading Math Readers, Step into Reading Phonics Readers, Step into Reading Write-In Readers and Step into Reading Phonics Boxed Sets—a complete literacy program with something to interest every child.

Learning to Read, Step by Step!

Ready to Read   Preschool–Kindergarten
• big type and easy words • rhyme and rhythm • picture clues
For children who know the alphabet and are eager to begin reading.

Reading with Help   Preschool–Grade 1
• basic vocabulary • short sentences • simple stories
For children who recognize familiar words and sound out new words with help.

Reading on Your Own   Grades 1–3
• engaging characters • easy-to-follow plots • popular topics
For children who are ready to read on their own.

Reading Paragraphs   Grades 2–3
• challenging vocabulary • short paragraphs • exciting stories
For newly independent readers who read simple sentences with confidence.

Ready for Chapters   Grades 2–4
• chapters • longer paragraphs • full-color art
For children who want to take the plunge into chapter books but still like colorful pictures.

STEP INTO READING® is designed to give every child a successful reading experience. The grade levels are only guides. Children can progress through the steps at their own speed, developing confidence in their reading, no matter what their grade.

Remember, a lifetime love of reading starts with a single step!

HERO STORY COLLECTION

RHUS26144

Published in the United States by Random House Children's Books, a division of Random House, Inc.,
1745 Broadway, New York, NY 10019, and in Canada by Random House of Canada Limited, Toronto.

Visit us on the Web!
StepIntoReading.com
randomhouse.com/kids
dckids.kidswb.com

Educators and librarians, for a variety of teaching tools, visit us at randomhouse.com/teachers

ISBN: 978-0-375-87298-3

MANUFACTURED IN CHINA

10 9 8 7 6 5 4 3 2

DC SUPER FRIENDS

HERO STORY COLLECTION

Step 1 and 2 Books

A Collection of Five Early Readers

Random House 🏠 New York

Contents

DC SUPER FRIENDS

FLYING HIGH

By Nick Eliopulos

Illustrated by Loston Wallace and David Tanguay

Random House 🏠 New York

Batman swings
over Gotham City.
The sun is shining.

But something
strange is in the air.
The Super Friends
have work to do.

Honk! Honk!

Pigeons block traffic.

The Flash races

to the rescue!

The pigeons
fly away.

Caw! Caw!

At the beach,

seagulls steal food.

19

Aquaman
and his friend

make a big splash!

Squawk!

Ostriches run away
from the zoo.

Superman and
Green Lantern
fly to the rescue!

They stop the birds
in their tracks.

Hmmm.

Batman spots a clue.

It is a strange machine.

Batman takes
a closer look.
The noisy machine
bothers the birds.

Now the birds
are happy again.

Inside, the Penguin
robs the bank.

"The Super Friends
are too busy!
They can't stop me,"
he says.

But Batman leaps

into action.

He stops

the Penguin's evil plan.

Teamwork
saves the day!

GOING BANANAS

By Benjamin Harper

Illustrated by Erik Doescher,
Mike DeCarlo, and David Tanguay

Random House New York

Metropolis is having
a gem show.

Everyone wants to see the big yellow diamond!

The diamond is gone!
Without it,
the show cannot open.

The Super Friends
will help!
They will find
the diamond.

Superman uses

his X-ray vision.

He finds a clue!

Green Lantern
finds another clue!
He spots
strange fingerprints.

Across town,
there is trouble
at the docks.

All the bananas are gone!
Batman, Robin,
and the Flash
are ready to help.

Batman spots
more strange
fingerprints!

Superman sees
more trouble.

A truck full of bananas
has been stolen!

Superman follows
the truck.
It races
down the city streets.

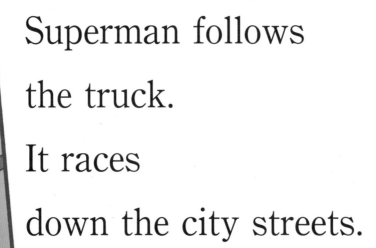

The truck stops.

A gorilla gets out!

Superman takes

a closer look.

It is Gorilla Grodd!
He is using a magic box,
the diamond, and
the bananas.

He is making
a magic
gorilla army.

53

"You are too late!"
Grodd says.

"My gorillas will
take over the city.
And then we will
take over the world!"

Gorillas go everywhere!

They run in the park.

They jump into the pond.

The Flash ties up
a gorilla
with rope!
Cyborg helps.

Gorillas run wild!

They make a mess.

Robin and Green Lantern
trap the gorillas.
They cannot go
anywhere!

Superman works fast.

The gorillas turn back
into bananas!
Batman captures Grodd!

Roar!

Grodd breaks free.

He grabs the diamond.

He escapes!

Superman chases Grodd.

He must not get away!

Gorilla Grodd hides

at the zoo.

Which gorilla has

the diamond?

Superman knows!

Growl!

Gorilla Grodd cannot
hide anymore.

He is taken away.

The Super Friends return
the diamond
just in time.
The show can go on.

The gem show is a hit—
thanks to
the Super Friends!

DC★SUPER FRIENDS™

BRAIN FREEZE!

By J. E. Bright

Illustrated by Loston Wallace and David Tanguay

Random House 🏠 New York

It is a big day
in Metropolis.

A new computer will control everything.

The computer
is called the Brain.
It will run the trains.

It will control
the traffic lights,
the water supply,
and the power.

Superman pulls
the switch that turns
on the Brain.

Mr. Freeze wants
to give Metropolis
brain freeze!

Mr. Freeze fires

his ice cannon.

The Brain is
frozen solid!

The city's water
stops running.

The power
goes off.

A train speeds

out of control!

Superman and the Flash
zoom into action.

Superman stops

the train.

The Flash helps

the riders.

Cyborg tells the cars when to STOP.

Green Lantern tells
them when to GO.

Batman swings down
on Mr. Freeze.

Mr. Freeze uses
his ice blaster!

Batman's feet
get frozen.

Superman breaks
the ice.

Batman smashes
the ice blaster.

Mr. Freeze runs

to his ice cannon!

Superman uses
his heat vision
to melt the cannon.

"Get ready to cool off in jail," Batman says.

Superman thaws

the Brain.

It still works!

Teamwork saves
the city.

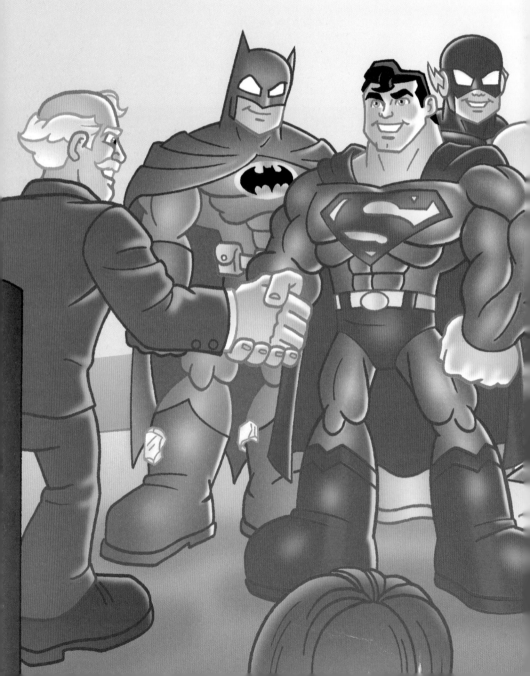

The Super Friends
celebrate
with ice cream!

DC SUPER FRIENDS™

T. REX TROUBLE!

By Dennis "Rocket" Shealy

Illustrated by Erik Doescher,
Mike DeCarlo, and David Tanguay

Random House 🏠 New York

Dinosaur fossils

are on parade.

Lex Luthor has a plan.

He sprays the T. rex

with his super foam.

Foam covers the bones.
The T. rex comes to life!

Lex rides the T. rex.

He makes more dinosaurs
come to life.

The pteranodon flies!

The triceratops stomps!

The Flash sees
the dinosaurs.

He calls the Super Friends.

The pteranodon
grabs the Flash.
The Flash cannot get
away.

The dinosaurs
scare the people.

Lex takes their money
and valuables.

The Super Friends arrive.

Batman says,

"Stop right there!"

Lex orders the dinosaurs to attack.

The dinosaurs charge
at the Super Friends!

Batman lassos
the triceratops.

The dinosaur bucks.
Batman holds on tight!

Green Lantern saves
the Flash with a tornado.

Green Lantern sets
the Flash safely on the
ground.

Superman fights
the T. rex.
Its mouth is
full of sharp teeth!

Superman keeps its jaws
from snapping shut!

Batman sees
a grocery truck.
He has an idea.

Batman steers
the triceratops
into the truck.

Meat and fish

pour out of the truck.

The dinosaurs
run to the food.

The pteranodon and
the T. rex start to eat.

The Flash grabs Lex!

Lex's plan has failed.
The Super Friends
have made friends
with the dinosaurs!

The Super Friends build
a home for the dinosaurs.
Everyone cheers!

STEP INTO READING®

STEP 2

DC SUPER FRIENDS

™

CRIME WAVE!

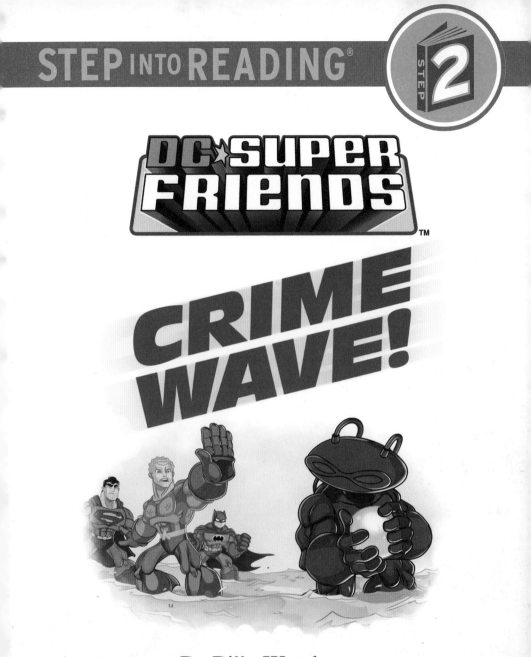

By Billy Wrecks

Illustrated by Dan Schoening

Random House New York

People are lining up
to see the world's
biggest pearl.

Aquaman cuts the ribbon
to open the show.
Superman, Batman,
and all the people cheer!

Suddenly, water floods in.

The people exit.

The Super Friends
help the people.

Tentacles rise

out of the water!

It is a giant octopus!

Black Manta rides a
shark into the room.
Electric eels spark
around him.

Black Manta

picks up the pearl.

He is stealing it!

The Super Friends stand
in Black Manta's way.

They will not let him

take the pearl.

Black Manta gives orders.
The shark, eels, and
octopus attack
the Super Friends.

The electric eels
chase Batman.
He swings toward
the penguin pen.

The water is freezing.

The eels trap Batman!

The shark snaps
at Aquaman!

Black Manta clutches
the pearl.

Superman fights
the octopus.

Black Manta

blasts Superman

with his lasers!

"I have won,"
Black Manta says.
"The pearl is <u>mine</u>!"

He forgets that Aquaman
can talk to sea creatures.

Aquaman tells

the octopus

that stealing is wrong.

The octopus sets

the Super Friends free.

Black Manta

falls backward.

A giant oyster clamps

down on his foot.

Black Manta is trapped.

Batman gets the pearl.

The police take

Black Manta away.

Batman and Aquaman
put the pearl back.

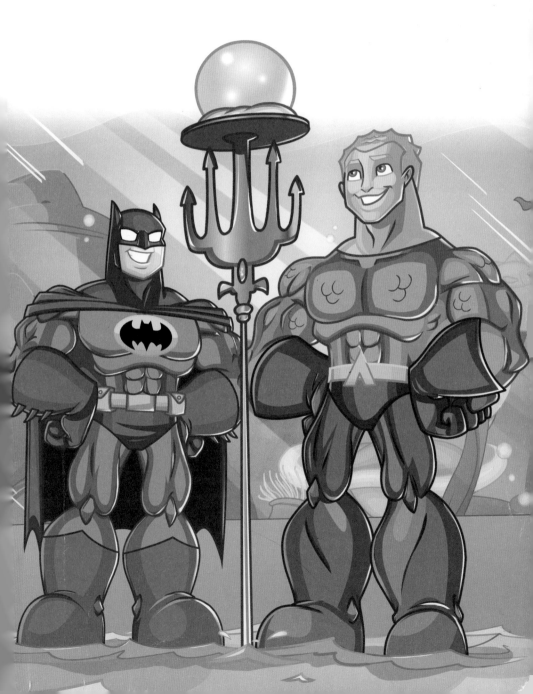

"I'm glad you are
on our side,"
Aquaman says.
"We don't have enough
Bat-Cuffs to arrest you!"